Hamish McHaggis

This book belongs to

...Ethan...Cooper...

.......Lots..of...love

Aunty Jilly, Uncle Graeme
x   x
Connor   & Gemma
x   x
BARNEY.
x

Publishing

www.gwpublishing.com

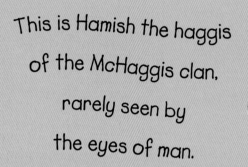

Hamish

This is Hamish the haggis
of the McHaggis clan,
rarely seen by
the eyes of man.

Rupert Harold the Third
is an English gent,
travelling far from
his home in Kent.

Rupert

Our Jeannie's an osprey with wide sweeping wings,
who is easily distracted by all sorts of things.

Jeannie

Angus

Young Angus is cheeky and likes playing the fool,
whatever he's doing he's got to look cool.

For Cara and Ian
with love. L.S.

For Luke with love. S.J.C.

www.lindastrachan.com
www.hamishmchaggis.com

First published in paperback in Great Britain 2008

Reprinted 2012

Design – Tony Fleetwood

Printed in China

Published by

GW Publishing
PO Box 15070
Dunblane
FK15 5AN

www.gwpublishing.com

ISBN 978-0-9554145-5-8

Hamish McHaggis

and

The Lost Prince

By Linda Strachan

Illustrated by Sally J. Collins

Hamish McHaggis was expecting a special visitor.

"She's on her way from Royal Deeside," he told Rupert. "There's been a bit of trouble with the wee Prince."

"A special visitor...? Royal Deeside...? A Prince...? Could it really be...!" Rupert wondered, as he admired his new bow tie in the mirror.

"I didn't know you knew such important people, Hamish. I've never met a ROYAL person before."

But Hamish wasn't listening. "Dearie me, this place is in a right mess. Angus! You've no put away your train set!"

"I'll do it later," Angus said, disappearing out the door.

Up in his favourite tree
Angus came nose to nose with a pretty red squirrel.
"Hello, I'm Angus," he said. "Who are you?

"Is this the McHaggis Hoggle?" she asked
breathlessly. "Does Hamish McHaggis bide here?"

"Aye, you're in the right place. **Hamish!** There's
someone to see you!" Angus called out.

Hamish rushed to the door of the Hoggle, but
Rupert got there first. He bowed low. "Welcome your
Maj... Oh! Who're you?"

"I see you found us," grinned Hamish.

"Is this your visitor?" Rupert whispered.
"I thought you meant…"

"Rupert, this is Shona, a good friend of mine. And here's Jeannie,
just in time. So, what's the matter with the Prince, now?"

"He's missing!" Shona told them. "He's been gone all
night and no one can find him."

"Aw, that's a sair fecht!" Jeannie fluttered her
feathers as she landed.

"Will you come and help us look for him?" Shona asked.

Hamish nodded quickly.

"Of course we will."

As soon as Shona left, Hamish ran back into the Hoggle and began raking about in his kist. "We'll need maps, compass and...."

"Watch out, Rupert!"

squeaked Jeannie as a pair of slippers went flying through the air. "Hamish, be careful."

"But I can't find my binoculars," Hamish grumbled.

"Here they are!" said Angus.

Hamish looked up. "That's grand! Now, as soon as I've packed my picnic basket we can load up the Whirry Bang and be off."

WATCH OUT!

The Whirry Bang clattered over the bridge to Balmoral.

Jeannie waved. "Look, there's Shona."

"Do you think we'll meet the Queen?" asked Rupert.

"Och, Rupert!" Hamish shook his head. "It's the Prince I'm concerned about. He's just wee and he's been out all night. His father will be worried sick. Listen, isn't that him calling?"

Bruaerk!

Bruaerk!

There was a deep throaty bark coming from the forest.

"But that sounds like a stag," Rupert corrected him.

"Of course it is," said Hamish. "That's the Monarch of the Glen, the young Prince's father."

"Oh, I see," said Rupert, looking embarrassed. "I thought it was a quite different Prince..."

"Everyone is gathering over there," Shona told them. Hamish and Jeannie followed her towards a large clearing in the forest.

"I'll be along in a moment," said Rupert. "I want to look at this map, first. That little deer could be anywhere."

"Hmmm," thought Angus.
"I bet I could see for miles
from the top of that tree.
Or maybe that one . . .
No, that other one is bigger
. . ."

He wandered off, deeper
and deeper into the woods.

Hamish organised the
animals into a search party
There were

rabbits,

a stoat,

two tiny shrews,

a wild cat,

grouse,

capercaillie,

a Highland cow
and her calf.

"I think we need a wee snack before we set off," said Hamish, opening his picnic basket.

But just then Rupert appeared. "I can't find Angus anywhere," he said. "He's wandered off into the forest. I bet he's got lost."

"Now we've two of them to find!" spluttered Hamish, through a mouthful of cucumber sandwich.

"Oh dear," said Shona. "Perhaps we should leave our picnic until after we've found them."

"Hello, up there!"

Angus looked down and saw a lady out walking
th her dogs.

"You must be a visitor," she said. "We've never had a
e marten with a red hat on the estate before."

"I'm Angus. I'm looking for the
young deer Prince. He's
lost," Angus told her.

"That's awfully good
of you. We will tell the
gamekeeper to keep a look out
for him too," she said.

"Goodbye, Angus."

Angus scampered off, deeper and deeper into the woods.

At first he thought it was great fun, but the tall trees soon hid most of the sunlight. He **jumped** at every strange sound.

The woods were

DARK

and

SPOOKY

As the wind whispered, rustling
through the leaves,
Angus felt as if eyes were
watching him through
the gloom.

Angus was feeling very scared and lonely. He was lost and the woods were so creepy. A sudden loud

crunch

made him jump.

It came from a large bramble bush behind him. He heard a strange snuffling noise, but what could it be? He crept carefully around the bush.

oh!

There, tangled in the jaggy brambles, was the wee Prince.

"Help! Please, can you help me?" he cried.

"I'm stuck and I've got a sore leg."

Angus helped him out of the bramble patch. He wrapped his clean handkerchief around the nasty scratch on the Prince's leg. "Would you like a drink of water?" he asked, gently.

"I want a bosie from my mum."

The little Prince looked as if he was trying hard not to cry.

"A bosie? Oh, a hug!"

Angus gave the Prince a cuddle and they both felt better.

"I'm going to climb to the top of that tree," Angus said, trying to sound very grown up. "I want to find the best way home." From the top of the tree he could see for miles.

"I can see the castle!"

Angus scampered back down to the wee prince.

It wasn't long before Angus found the path that led them home.

Hamish and the other animals were searching for Angus and the wee Prince. They came out into a wide clearing just as Angus and the Prince emerged from the woods on the other side.

"There they are!" Jeannie flew over to check they were both safe and well.

"I found him!"
Angus told them.

"All by myself!"

"Thank you very much for finding our wee Prince, Angus," said the Monarch of the Glen.

"I think we should have a party to celebrate!" said Shona.

Later, everyone agreed that it was one of the best parties anyone at Balmoral could remember.

'Look! Up on the hill," said Jeannie. " It's the wee Prince and his family."

"You know," Angus told Rupert, "when I was in the woods I
met a nice lady and her corgi dogs."
Rupert stared at Angus." You... you ... you met... her Majesty?"
Angus just grinned.

DID YOU KNOW?

Coorie doon means to nestle or cosy down comfortably.

Braw means good.

Blether means to gossip or chatter.

To bide means to live in a place.

It's a sair fecht means it's a terrible time or a worry.

A bosie is a hug or a cuddle.

A kist is a large box or trunk.

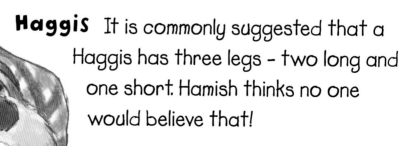

Haggis It is commonly suggested that a Haggis has three legs - two long and one short. Hamish thinks no one would believe that!

Young **Pine Martens** have yellow-white fur, which changes to grey, and then to brown as they mature.

A **Hedgehog** may have up to 5000 spines. The rest of its body is covered with brown fur.

An **Osprey** is able to close its nostrils to stop water getting up its nose when it dives for fish.

Red Squirrels collect mushrooms and store them in trees.

Red Deer get their name from their red fur, but in winter they grow a thicker grey-brown coat for extra warmth.

Balmoral has been the Scottish home of the Royal Family since 1848.

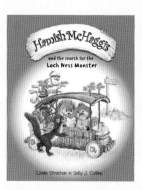

**Hamish McHaggis
and The search for The
Loch Ness Monster**

978-0-9546701-5-3

**Hamish McHaggis
and The Edinburgh Adventure**

978-0-9546701-7-7

**Hamish McHaggis
and The Ghost of Glamis**

978-0-9546701-9-1

**Hamish McHaggis
and The Skye Surprise**

978-0-9546701-8-4

**Hamish McHaggis
and The Skirmish at Stirling**

978-0-9551564-1-0

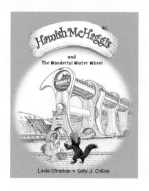

**Hamish McHaggis
and The Wonderful Water Wheel**

978-0-9551564-0-3

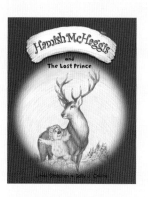

**Hamish McHaggis
and The Wonderful Water Wheel**

978-0-9554145-5-8

**Hamish McHaggis
and The Clan Gathering**

978-0-9561211-2-7

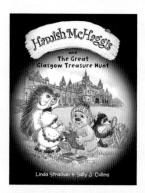

**Hamish McHaggis
and The Great
Glasgow Treasure Hunt**

978-0-9570844-0-7

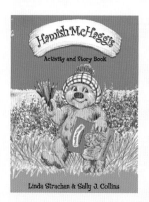

**Hamish McHaggis
Activity and Story Book**

978-0-9554145-1-0

Also by the
same author
and illustrator

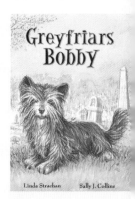

Greyfriars Bobby

978-0-9551564-2-7